Wo... Are Our Friends

Written by Kenneth Peacock
Illustrated by Mary Lou Peacock

MW01243946

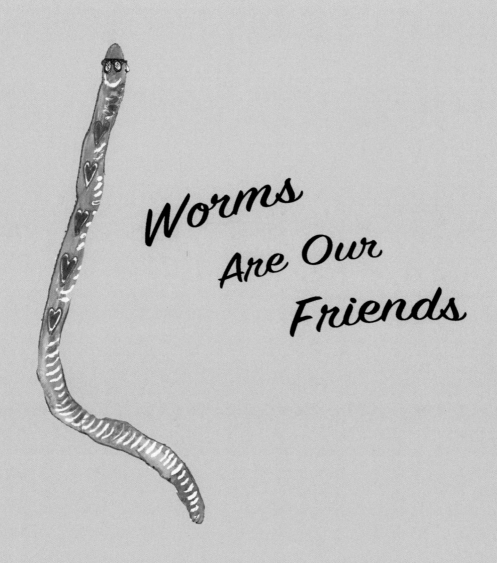

Worms
Are Our
Friends

Written by Kenneth Peacock
Illustrated by Mary Lou Peacock

Worms Are Our Friends

This is a fun filled Children's book about the importance of our Worm Buddies in the preparation of the soil to grow all plants.

It explains how worms actually nourish and naturally fertilize the soil.

You will learn many fun facts that a lot of people are not aware of about our Worm Buddies.

Written by Kenneth Peacock
Illustrated by Mary Lou Peacock

© 2021 Kenneth Peacock

WORMS ARE OUR FRIENDS

Worms are our really good friends.
In fact, I am going to tell you why of all the creatures
in the ground we think we are Number 1.

I HAVE A VERY FUN JOB.
I so enjoy what I do every day.
I am going to let you in on what I do to help prepare
the soil with the best nutrition to grow healthy
fruits, vegetables and all plants.

DO YOU KNOW WHAT DIRT IS?

It's just dead soil until it can come alive.
Every day my worm family plays a big part
to help nourish the soil, which nourishes the roots,
which in turn will nourish our plants,
which will nourish everyone. This is why worms are
important for much of plant growth.

I will be talking more about why the worms are so very important
for the preparation of our soil to feed all plant life on land.
Before we discuss this further let's talk more about some
very interesting facts about our worm buddies.

DO YOU KNOW THAT THERE ARE APPROXIMATELY 2,700 DIFFERENT KINDS OF WORMS?

In fact, in one acre of land there could be
one million worms.
One acre is almost the size of a football field.

WORMS HAVE A LOT OF HEART

In fact, we have 5 hearts!!

I guess the reason we have 5 hearts is
because we put a lot of *LOVE*
in what we do each day.

Another interesting fact about our worm families
is that we have no arms, legs or eyes.
We do have light receptors
and can tell if we are in the dark or in the light.

We have a microscopic antenna shaped sensor
at the tip of our head.
This helps us to know where
we are and to navigate ourselves underground.

THE WORMS AERATE THE SOIL.

By this we mean the worms
travel through the soil and make little tunnels.
Worms have mouths that allow us to chew and digest
dirt and nutrients found in the soil as we are tunneling
through the soil. This allows oxygen and
rain water to be absorbed into the soil.

Rain water also provides oxygen molecules
to help the roots of the plants to grow big and strong.
We also will leave behind as we tunnel,
castings or commonly called *"Worm Poop"*.

This "Worm Poop" will fertilize the soil.
In fact, many farmers that use the castings
refer to them as *Black Gold.*

In addition to eating the soil, we will eat leaves and grasses.
We also will enjoy living in a compost pile
made up of kitchen scraps such as;
vegetables, some fruits (especially bananas and melons).
Worms can eat and digest half our body weight each day.

We also like ground up eggshells, wood chips, newspaper, dead leaves and coffee grounds.

We think that sometimes we are a little picky as some of us don't like onions.

Another interesting fun fact about worms
is how we breathe.
Worms breathe in oxygen and let carbon dioxide out,
just like people but we do not have lungs.
We do not breathe through our mouth
and certainly can't breathe through our nose
because we don't have a nose.
We breathe through our skin.
Worms must stay moist to breathe.
If we become too dry, we will suffocate and die.
However, after a hard rain the tunnels
that worms have made will be flooded with water.
You will often see many worms
coming out of the ground and on driveways,
because worms cannot get enough oxygen to breathe.
Some of the worms become disoriented
and are not able to get
back in the ground.

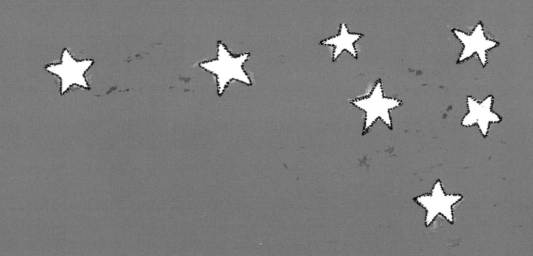

Worms do not like the light
and try to avoid
being in the light.

Sometimes certain worms are called
'NIGHT CRAWLERS'
because they will come out
at night.

Worms live where there is food,
moisture, oxygen and favorable temperature.
Let me tell you about how worms reproduce.
Worms will reproduce by laying a
lemon shaped yellow cocoon.
In each cocoon, there will be many tiny eggs.
Depending on environment and weather
these tiny eggs could hatch
in as little as 3-6 weeks.
The worms can double their population
in 2-3 months.
Earth worms have no ears
but their bodies can sense the vibrations
of any creatures for their protection
from any predators.

Another interesting fact about our worm castings
is that you can make
a worm casting *"Tea"* out of worm poop.
Farmers and home gardeners are finding out
that this "Tea" is valuable to help produce very healthy
vegetables and fruits that taste delicious.

Gardeners apply this "Tea" directly
on the ground and also apply this liquid
to the foliage above ground to the leaves and stems.
They usually dilute the "Tea" with purified water
or rain water using either a sprayer or a watering can.

They make this worm "Tea" by putting worm castings
(worm poop) and compost into a painter's
strainer bag or burlap bag.
The farmers place this bag suspended in a bucket or
barrel of water depending on how much they are
going to need for their garden.
Then place an air stone in the container, which is like
a fish tank filter to put oxygen in the water
making bubbles. The moving water will make the life
in the castings and compost come alive.

These very tiny or microscopic creatures that will
come alive in this "Tea" will be poured out on the plants.
The "Tea" which we also call brew will feed the
roots and soil. Then the web of life which is in the soil
will also become nourished by this "Tea".
Now this web of life in the soil will really become
super charged and create very healthy plants
and tasty vegetables.

In the beginning of our book we mentioned
how the worm casting or "Worm Poop"
naturally fertilizes the soil
which is able
to feed the roots,
which in turn
feeds the plants,
which in turn
feeds us.

*THIS IS WHY OUR
WORM BUDDIES
ARE TRULY OUR FRIENDS.*

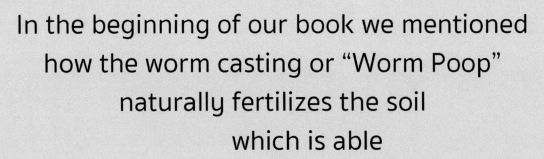

Author Kenneth Peacock
is thankful
for his Worm Buddies to
help make his gardens grow.

Made in the USA
Middletown, DE
24 October 2023

40573069R00015